Chill

In memory of Brian Anson, friend, artist and storyteller.

Little Hare Books
an imprint of
Hardie Grant Egmont
85 High Street
Prahran, Victoria 3181, Australia
www.littleharebooks.com

National Library of Australia
Cataloguing-in-Publication entry

Thompson, Carol.
Chill / Carol Thompson.
9781921541735 (hbk.)
For pre-school age.
823.914

Designed by Vida and Luke Kelly
Produced by Pica Digital Ltd, Singapore
Printed through Phoenix Offset
Printed in Shen Zhen, Guangdong Province, China, April 2010

5 4 3 2 1

Chill

Words and illustrations
by Carol Thompson

LITTLE HARE
www.littleharebooks.com

Dolly likes to play on her own.

Dum-di-dum-di-dum!

Especially the mirror game.

But some games are not much fun all alone.

Then ...

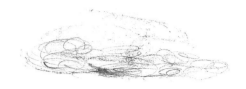

along comes Jack Rabbit,

Dolly's best friend in all the world.

Some days Jack and Dolly
are quiet together.
They go to their Best Place
and watch the clouds.

Or listen to their favourite music.

Some days they race around so fast

and play so hard,

all they can do is . . .

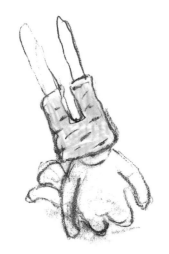

LAUGH!

Jacky Knotty Noodle!

Dolly Wolly Doodle!

One day, when Dolly went to visit
Jack, he was wearing a beret.

Jack painted a big circle.
And then some smaller circles.
Dolly painted some long wobbly lines.

Dolly looked at Jack's picture.

Jack looked at Dolly's picture.

He's not my friend.

Jack's wrong.

I'm SAD ...

She's not
my friend.

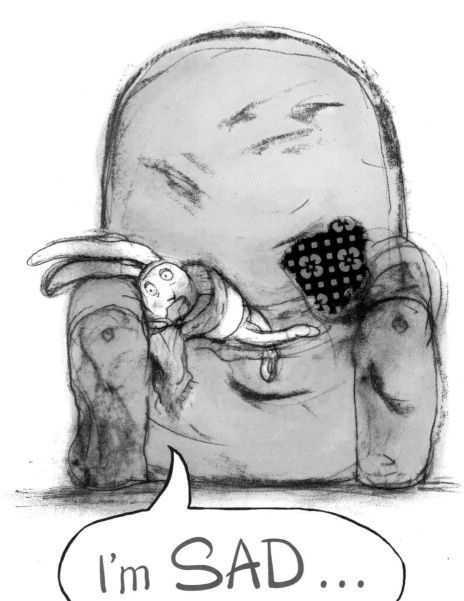

I'm SAD ...

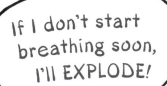

Dolly takes a deep breath.
All the way in and all the way out.

Dolly takes a
lovely warm bath.
She closes her
eyes and thinks
of something she
likes a lot.

If I don't stop thinking about that Dolly soon, I'll EXPLODE!

Jack counts slowly up to ten,
and back down again.
And up again!

Aaaaahhhhh!

He closes his
eyes and thinks
of something he
likes a lot.

The next day . . .

Dolly goes to her Best Place.

Jack goes to his Best Place.